Commodified I am so confused
I have no head for money but
my mouth is a coin slot.
With blood tang metal on my tongue
there is nothing I can swallow

COUNtRY GIRL::3
THe DeBUtaNtE::4
LoVe LaNGUage::23
haRVeSt MOON::24
HoMeSiCK::25
sUMmER NiGhT CiTy::26
MiD yEaR ReViEw::27
coUSinS::28
EuRoStaR sALe::29
chaRiTaBLe iNtERpRetaTioN::30
coLDeR LiGHT::31
i ThoUgHt i WaNt To SeE tHe SeA::32
FoReSt aNgeL::41
LatE spRiNg::42
faLLiNg mAn::43
hELLs iN BoTTLes::44
RusH houR::45
buToH CLaSs::46
a HoRizOn SheDS iTseLF::47
LiNeS iN tHe SaNd::48
juNiPeR::49
GgGirL!!!::50

mAteRiaL::51
fLoaTiNg::52
rEviSiOniSt hiStoRiEs Of loVe::54
sOFT coRe::57
ComE spRinG::58
dUES::59
rAbBit yEaR::60
eVeLyN::61
mUd::62
StRayS::64
ReMemBeR tHe hErBs mY LoVe::65
SLeEp kNiFe::66
moOnY MeAL::67
MeaLy MoON::68
neEdLeSs::69
EArLy BrEAkFaSt::70
seALaNt::71
LoNg LiVe DrEaMy dopPeLgäNgERs::72
eXcALiBuR::75
BLOSsOm::76
seEdBiRd::77
dOe::78
TOp SEaSoN::79
RecOvery::80
aNTisEpTic::81
FeBRuAry 2012::82
sTrATeGEm::83
ReTroGrAde::84
hUsK::85

aLl RightS ReSerVed

phOtoS :: kaisa SaARiNen

© 2024 kAiSa sAaRiNeN

isBn :: 979-8-9900257-1-4

bOok dEsigN :: StEve BaRbARo

reQuests FOR rePrOductioN oF any & ALL paRts oF tHis BooK shOuLd be diRected To :: newSinewsmag@GmAiL.cOm

mAiToNauT::

mAiToNauT::

mAiToNauT::

mAiToNauT::

mAiToNauT::

mAiToNauT::

mAiToNauT::

mAiToNauT::

mAiToNauT::

mAiToNauT::

mAiToNauT::

mAiToNauT::

mAiToNauT::

mAiToNauT::

mAiToNauT::

mAiToNauT::

mAiToNauT::

::mAiTONauT

::mAiTONauT

::mAiTONauT

::mAiTONauT

::mAiTONauT

::mAiTONauT

::mAiTONauT

::mAiTONauT

::mAiTONauT

::mAiTONauT

::mAiTONauT

::mAiTONauT

::mAiTONauT

::mAiTONauT

::mAiTONauT

::mAiTONauT

bY kAiSa SAaRiNeN

Country Girl

Beneath the milky blue sun, scalding sky
Gravel path exhales dust in little clouds
Embraced by the golden symmetry of wheat fields
The bondage of beauty to eternity
Leaves me gasping for air under apple trees

I sink into spilt milk until it clogs my heart
Until I have fed myself all of my foetid sorrows
Fat lactose streaks running down my cheeks
Until I have swallowed every drop and learned to love
My medicine, grazing on this little regret and that

Red autumn enters the body like a milk fever
Deep in the fields a barn self-immolates
Ripening into the point of collapse, ghosts roam the landscape
Holding petrol cans and torn porno magazines
We play hide and seek in a stairwell full of nails

I am alive and I see beyond the nights!
Decay makes nature a true mirror
Fruit flesh sticks to my soles, a second skin
I find the blade hidden in every caress
Counting blood cells in the milk of kindness

The Debutante

Cutting through the crowds of Center Gai, I still feel like an insect. Part of a swarm, a plague on this shining city. Up on the LCD screen, a singing girl rounds her pink lips. It's a perfect O for Otherworldly. I am a cicada preparing to molt, a pearly shell forming around my skin as I ascend toward the special girl.

I step into the Tower building elevator and find another teenager there, quite like me: dressed in a navy blue school uniform, baby-faced but skinny, an endearing bruise on one of her bony knees. I got mine from falling in the bathroom, desperately drunk. Hers are probably from PE class in the private school she attends, leagues above my level. Her skin looks like make-up would be an insult to it. She is too far away to even notice me staring at her.

We get off on the same floor, wordlessly. My heart quickens as I trail her down a long corridor. It would not surprise me if she was signed to the same label; she seems to belong in this world much more than I do. I know she must be a newcomer like me, because I would know her if she had already debuted, but the thought is not reassuring. She has molted a long time ago, or perhaps entered this world already possessing her skin, ready to wield the body like a blade.

As I expected --- feared --- hoped? her stride comes to a halt at the door of Mr. Takahata, my manager. She hesitates for a second before knocking. 'Come in,' Mr. Takahata shouts. She enters without holding the door open for me. I wonder if she genuinely has not noticed my presence. Perhaps I have turned into a ghost with a heartbeat. For a split second I close my eyes and let myself float in the glittering dream.

'Ah, Suzuka, you're on time for once,' Mr. Takahata says. 'Come take a seat.'

I keep my head half-bowed as I sit beside the elevator girl. She looks at me as though only becoming aware of my existence for the first time, taking in every wrinkle on my clothes, every strand of hair out of place. Pinned under her full attention, I am so close to insecthood.

'Don't look so confused,' Mr. Takahata says, jovially, to both of us. 'Yukiko, this is Suzuka. Suzuka, Yukiko.'

'Pleased to meet you, Suzuka,' Yukiko says, bowing. Her voice is clear but sweet, crystallized honey, exactly how a girl's voice should be. Mine sounds all wrong --- not genderless, but the singular cry of a failed girl. I press my lips together.

'You're both slated to debut this November, so I thought it'd be good for you girls to meet.'

We nod in unison, and it elevates me.

'Yukiko is our most recent signee. In fact, she was only contracted last week. She is incredibly impressive --- plays three instruments, dances well, face and voice of an angel.'

'Ah, please --- ' Yukiko giggles, hiding her mouth behind a thin hand.

'We have no doubt your debut will be a hit. Suzuka, on the other hand...She's been signed to us for a full two years now, but we're still getting her ready for the debut.'

'A diamond takes some time to refine,' Yukiko says sweetly.

'So you're a diplomat.'

They giggle conspiratorially, and I have nothing to say to defend myself.

'You'll be sharing your TV debut in December's Shinrai Shoujo program. Rehearsals start next Tuesday.'

'How exciting,' Yukiko sighs.

'Yes, I'm looking forward to it,' I say. I just want to go home and bury my head in a pillow, put the TV on loud, but I am still here, nodding involuntarily as Mr. Takahata explains something I do not follow. It probably does not even really concern me. Not a single word of the subsequent conversation manages to stab through the static in my head, until we are finally being dismissed.

'I'll see you in the fitting tomorrow, Yukiko --- make sure not to eat too much breakfast.' Mr. Takahata glances at me and says, by way of goodbye, 'Just don't get yourself into any more trouble, Suzuka.'

My big sister is a yo-yo dieting nurse, and she sometimes sends me scrubs that don't fit her right. I love wearing them at home and pretending I'm in a hospital. What I really want is to be cared for, tucked into bed and given pills that give me dreamless sleep, but the vague medical associations are enough to satisfy my naïve heart. While wearing her clothes, I often dream of my big sister. I am lying in the darkness, an IV tube in my arm, and she emerges from a square of pure light, drawing the curtains of my bed apart. She brings me trays of citrus fruits, pets my hair and takes my temperature. She sings lullabies into my ear and whispers gossip about the old people in our hometown. Her body is warm and firm like the earth. Every time, I wake up smiling.

I'm not sleepy enough to coax my sister into taking care

of me, yet, so I lie on top of my bed covers and listen to the sound of traffic below, the inane talk show blaring on TV, my phone vibrating with relentless notifications. My apartment is small and dirty, but I can always settle in the labyrinthine house of loneliness. On TV, the ad break segues into the theme song of Hundred Princess, and I lift my head up to stare at the screen. This week, the main performers are the B group of YZW68. I recognize most of these girls, and they're all quite boring. The interview segment drags on for far too long.

'What's your favorite animal, Sayuri-chan?'

'Um, I like cats.'

'What do you like about cats?'

'Well --- they're so cute! Aren't they?'

'What about you, Mika-chan?'

'I like cats too.'

Their dance number is equally lifeless, anemic marionettes defeated by their calorie deficits. True professionals would know how to power through. I can't see any of them being promoted to the A group anytime soon. Overcome with frustration, I switch the TV off before the credits roll. My fingers clench and unclench around the silver handles of the sewing scissors kept in a plastic box under my bed, together with other supplies. I know I've got to stop it with the cutting. If only I knew who ratted me out to Mr. Takahata, I would cut that bitch instead. But I've got to let it go. The scars on my thigh are almost faded, and there will be no new ones.

'What if your debut is a failure, and you end up going the gravure route?' Mr. Takahata had asked me after he found out, not unreasonably. 'Who's gonna want to see a maimed chick in a bikini?' He had fallen silent for a while before adding: 'Actually, I'm sure there's a market for that.' I know there is --- I've watched the stuff. Still, I got the message. There is some hope for me yet. Mr. Takahata might not have much faith in me, but neither is he in a hurry to discard me, and I know I should be grateful for that.

Sometimes, in my more cynical moments, I wonder if there truly is that much of a difference between the dream-worlds of the idol, the gravure model, even the AV starlet. In each case, a girl carries the expectations of an audience, sublimates herself through them, all the way to eternity --- a glossy page, a shining screen, a sticky half-memory. I know I can only think this way because I am a pervert. For most people, there exists a difference of morals. Therefore, no cutting for me. I roll over in bed and stare at my wall, my screen, my wall, my screen, my wall, drag myself out of bed and stare at my physics homework. Ambulances scream by as I calculate movements of kinetic energy. My own body is so sluggish, barely generating any heat at all, numbed by boredom and hunger pangs. I know a mission exists for me in this world, but I have not been set upon it just yet.

Because of last summer's incident and my old cutting habit, Mr. Takahata seems convinced I am suicidal, which is an insult. The one time I did try to kill myself, the goal was not to die, and I thought it would be fairly obvious to everyone who should've known me. I was simply tired of waiting, being muzzled with an impotent contract. I have no memories of the hours following my admittance to the hospital; I woke up from a total blackout with a drip in my arm.

'Mr. Takahata from Dove Heart is here to see you,' a nurse had said by way of greeting, already opening the door to let him in.

Mr. Takahata looked haggard, as though my incident had kept him up all through those hours I swam in the sea of chemical sleep. 'Good morning, princess,' he'd said, a wry smile on his face. 'I was wondering if you'd sleep for a hundred years.' At that point, my head still felt very heavy, and even a gentle shake of it had sent ripples of nausea through my body.

'Morning,' I'd said simply, trying to move my face as little as possible.

'Do you remember the voicemail you sent last night?'

'No.'

'Shall I recount what you said?'

'Please.'

'You said you'll kill yourself unless I let you have your debut by the end of the year. The call from the hospital reached me earlier than your message.' He'd paused for a moment, laughing dryly to himself. 'Fuck, I thought. Is this really it? Are you really so impatient? Naturally I rushed here, and they said you just OD'd on over-the-counter painkillers. They had to pump your stomach, but there's no sign of liver damage.' He'd taken a very deep smoker-wheeze of a breath. 'Look, Suzuka-san. I am simply confused. What do you want from me, from this life? Do you really want to die?'

'What I said in my voicemail was true,' I'd said, my voice thin but confident enough. 'I don't remember it, but I must have meant every single word. You have to give me this. Otherwise I swear I will jump from the roof of the hospital.'

'Please consider this from my perspective,' he'd said. 'If you're going to pull stunts like this, how are we supposed to trust you as an employee?'

'I don't care if you trust me or not. If you don't give me a real chance, I'm going to off myself. That's a promise.'

That made him laugh again, more nervously. 'Look, kid, I'll see what I can do for you. Just stay away from the roof for now. Will you promise that too?'

I'd nodded and been left alone in the strange unsanitary loneliness of the hospital. I spent seven days there, being monitored for signs of further mental imbalance. I suppose I might have been let out sooner, had the record label wanted me. During those muggy afternoons, staring at the grey stage curtain of the July sky, my mind was cloudless. I was counting down the hours to hear the verdict from the label: would they give me something to live for? In the end, my debut single was penciled in, circled in red on my pocket calendar. Mr. Takahata came to bring me a new outfit, a maroon dress with a V-neck that accentuated my collarbones and the slope of my neck. At first, I thought it was simply a gift to lift my spirits, but it turned out to be a stage direction. Magazine photographers were waiting for me as I left the hospital. It was July 19th, the first day of my life.

Now, summer is long gone, and the exhilaration of rebirth is starting to give way to a new anxiety: what if my new life is stillborn after all? Perhaps I have been caught red-handed, trying to steal something that was never supposed to belong to me. If it was going to happen, wouldn't it have happened without me forcing it, pulling the trigger? I am already being pushed aside by younger, prettier, more talented girls. I could see it in Yukiko's eyes --- she could tell I would never amount to anything. She was kind enough to treat me with civility, perhaps compelled with a certain kind of noblesse oblige.

My phone screen lights up with an incoming call from Mr. Takahata, prompting me to drop the pen I've been absent-mindedly holding onto. 'Hello. What's the matter?'

'Suzuka-chan. Something has come up --- an interesting opportunity. Can you come into the office so we can discuss it in private?'

'Right now?'

'As soon as possible.'

I take off the scrubs and fold them carefully over my chair. They'll wait for my return. I put on a black velvet turtleneck and a pleated gingham miniskirt, even though I'd prefer to wear the navy dress I barely wore the night before. In the months following my dramatic discharge, the paparazzi have mostly lost their interest, but on slow gossip days, they occasionally latch onto me for things like repeating outfits. It matches the persona they've given me --- a tasteless country girl who's lost her way in the city, out of her depth and her mind. Every time I hand them some easy material, it stings, but I reason they might just as well invent it from thin air. I could barricade myself into my apartment for months and see headlines decrying my secret affair with a married actor pop up from the ether. It's all just a game, and I know I'll never win, so the best I can do is lose with grace.

A cold rain is falling, ghostly in the flare of street lamps.

I hold onto my umbrella with a white-knuckled grip. The station is quiet; rush hour is over. I wonder if every other person on the platform is thinking of throwing their body on the gleaming wet tracks, too. In most cases, thinking horrible thoughts is actually a protective mechanism. It is normal for new parents to think about throwing their baby down the stairs, or for car drivers to obsess over the idea of swerving into the wrong lane. The purpose of catastrophizing is to prepare you for the real thing, should the universe be cruel enough.

On the train, I hold the wet umbrella close to my chest. By Ikenoue station, my turtleneck is soaked through with rainwater, and my teeth are chattering. Old women give me strange looks. I feel completely absorbent.

The moment the elevator stops at the Dove Heart floor, I feel an overwhelming urge to go back, smash the ground floor button, run away, disappear. The storm is a cliché of a bad omen, but it's a classic. Slowly, the door slides open to reveal the familiar sight of the bright-lit and perfumed offices. I hesitate for a split second before running down the corridor to Mr. Takahata's office.

'Come in,' he says before I have even knocked.

Mr. Takahata always looks as though God was being frugal with skin while making him. There's not quite enough of it to cover his skull comfortably, so it pulls tight over his sharp nose and his protruding cheekbones. Even his lips are too thin, barely framing his mouth. This evening, he somehow looks even more severe than usual, his spindling fingers wrapping tight around a glass of whiskey.

'Take a seat, Suzuka-san.'

'What's wrong?'

'Oh, nothing is wrong --- as I said over the phone, it is an opportunity.'

'A good opportunity?'

He scoffs. 'An opportunity is a good thing by definition. Don't be silly.'

'I suppose,' I offer and wait for him to tell me more. He empties his glass and stares down at it before pouring himself another fat finger.

'Some opportunities involve more risks than others,' he finally continues. 'But all are good.'

'I agree,' I say. 'Can you tell me more about this opportunity?'

'That's what I called you here for. It has to do with your debut.'

My heart crashes so fast it's painful, and I exhale. It was

never going to happen. They're going to sideline me --- maybe give me a gravure gig. My mouth is glued shut. At least there is a way out. There is always a way out.

'Don't worry,' Mr. Takahata says. 'It's still going to happen. Just in a slightly different format.'

'What do you mean?' I exhale.

'It's actually quite exciting. The label wants to pioneer a new format called self-edge cloud-base. In this medium, your music will express the true nature of your soul, interpreted from your dreamwaves. You will perform in an eternal capacity.'

'I don't understand.'

'Your consciousness will be transferred into the cloud, and you will retain your full agency, existing in a digital format.'

'I will only exist in a digital format?'

He nods and smiles, impressed that I'm finally keeping up.

'What will happen to my body?'

'Well, it becomes irrelevant. Isn't that a blessing?'

'Are you telling me I should finish what I started?'

'I would never put it like that. We are not talking about suicide.'

'How do you want me to do it?'

'Slow down. First, we must make careful preparations, precisely because this has nothing to do with suicide. Your consciousness must be extracted before or at the moment your body ceases functioning.'

The words ring through my head like screams across the surface of a clear lake. The dream of becoming an idol is a dream of sacrifice: giving away your humanity to the eternal image. Some girls are too afraid to reach this conclusion, and I can always tell. I have never been afraid. I know I was born for this purpose, the veil already thrown over me, separating my hazy, barely-there self from the lucid, emotionless image of me. I know I have the right constitution; my problem is that my image is not yet beautiful enough. If it was a question of devotion, nobody could beat me.

'Suzuka-san?'

'Sorry.'

'How do you feel?'

I shake my head slightly. 'It doesn't matter. I want this. I won't back out.'

'That's excellent,' Mr. Takahata says, staring out into the wet black night. I count the burst veins in his eyes.

'That's it, then,' I say. 'For my life.'

He looks at me with a wistful kind of smile on his face. 'For your old life. It hasn't exactly been dancing on roses, anyway, has it?'

In that moment, I think he looks like my father, even though I know he does not. My father was a short, stocky, red-faced man; Mr. Takahata is pencil-thin and pale, waning in sight. Their appearances hardly matter. I always find fathers in the men hell-bent on destroying me.

On the train ride home, I stare at my reflection in the rain-washed windows, looking for God. Is he offering me salvation? Is this madness a sign of his absence? My face is a half-gone memory imprinted on the glass.

The rain has stopped. As I navigate neon lit puddles, my phone chimes with the opening chords of Parallelisme. It's my sister --- the only person whose calls I answer, save for Mr. Takahata.

'Is everything OK?'

My sister rarely calls.

'I just wanted to check if you're still coming home for New

Year's. Has the label confirmed your schedule yet?'

'I'm not going to be on Kouhaku, if that's what you're angling for. Of course I'm coming home.'

'OK. That's all.'

'See you. Bye.'

The door of my apartment clicks shut behind me. I walk into the living room without turning on the lights. This place does not feel mine anymore; neither does my body. I am watching a train crash into someone else's house, so close the flames lick my skin, but they are lukewarm. On TV, my label mate with a wildly successful sophomore single still fresh in his rearview mirror is taking a long swig of water. His forehead shimmers with sweat. 'The next song is for Nana,' he says and flashes a smile that could power Yoyogi Stadium for a week. He and his new fiancée have been in the eye of a minor media storm for the past week or two. They're both young, pretty, in the business --- a foolproof recipe for deranged backlash. Somehow, I expected Aoki's masculinity would save him, but I was naïve. He's been called a cradle-robber, a gold-digging rentboy, a walking dildo with an inflamed ego, and worse. Still, he's out on the stage, while Nanami is lying low, waiting out her days as an unmarried woman.

The audience's applause makes Aoki wince, as though the sound is wounding him. I don't feel too bad for him.

However anxious he may be in that moment, showing a brave front to the world, he has someone waiting for him at home.

I put on the navy blue dress, fix my hair with a silver barrette, and step out again. I consider going to Omotesando and spending my savings on a couple of designer dresses, going out like a firework, but all I really want is a seat at a smoky izakaya, a stack of greasy plates beside me.

'Keep a low profile until the extraction,' Mr. Takahata said. 'We still want you to go to the rehearsal on Tuesday. Don't cause a scene. Don't do anything out of the ordinary. When it happens, it will shock the whole world into loving you.'

The izakaya is half-empty, and I get a seat at a secluded booth near the back. I was almost hoping to get seated at the counter, to be noticed, pierced with eyes. What is a girl like me doing, eating like a pig? Trying to fill in the cracks in my heart? In the end, it hardly matters whether the voices come from the outside.

After finishing up a milky bowl of ramen, I order fried aubergines, their bellies glazed with sweet miso. My stomach pushes against the tight cradle of the dress. After that, half a dozen chicken skewers. After that, a plate of deep-fried tofu in a dark golden broth. Light-headed with salt and grease, I cross the street and enter a bright-lit dessert café. I buy a massive slice of chocolate cake, finish half and take the rest of it home in a pretty little cardboard box. I wonder if the box is heavier than the one my ashes will be placed in. What will my sister think of its weight when she carries me home for the new year?

I don't ask what exactly will happen to my body. I assume it will be neat, clinical, resembling a scene from documentaries about Swiss euthanasia clinics. No jumping from a tenth-story window, no blood-speckled windshields, no traumatized passersby. My corpse will be well-preserved for incineration. As for my mind, I do not know. When the door clicks shut behind me and I am in the darkness again, a wave of fear swirls inside me. They will decipher every part of me: stray thoughts disinterred from the mud of time; imperfect half-circles of unfinished realizations; memories of innocence; shameful secrets --- my own and those I keep; desires I do not acknowledge or understand. Will they understand why I need to go through this, better than I do? Will they think I'm beautiful? I flip the light switch.

Love Language

How many animals has your mother killed
And were they large and soft-skinned
Did her teeth shine red in the moonlight
And did the needle tremble in her hand
How many animals has your mother killed
A carcass at the throne of the Sunday table
Garlands of flesh on your golden hair
How many animals has your mother killed
The gun so cold against the sow's forehead
Breathing in unison, out, in, then silence
Until the squelch of boots against mud
How many animals has your mother killed
I never saw her in white, save for a wedding photo
Torn in half, her face turned towards the grave
Feeding daddy with sweet flowers
How many animals has your mother killed
And did she ever stick a wooden cross into the earth
Ever rock a small body into that cradle of clay
The wet salt of fear like expensive perfume
Did she recognise in their darkening eyes
The cascade of dying days. And how many
Has your mother killed so you don't have to
Because the pain is either here or it is there
Where the graves can stay unmarked
And there is no language for mourning

Harvest Moon

The magpie spread its jet black wings
Atop the wedding cake
Tilling soft fields of buttercream
The bride looked away, bloodshot

Red flags hung heavy from the ceiling
Tongues licking the dust of time
Preserving digits without memory

The violator caught a virgin gleam
Sterling silver on her finger
Barely costlier than garden soil

Dark feathers fell over all eyes
Bitter ash, barren heart, the beak
Glowed with silent curses

In seven moonlit murders
The guests took their leave
Flying out of the old union hall

The bride gazed at the butcherbird
Her uninvited guest of honour
The ruined cake, slash and burn
Hoping something new would grow

I miss feeling fruit flesh underfoot
In the yard spilling over with weeds and damsons
Getting drunk on the scent alone

Maybe I can only see what is already inside of me
It is true that I love a circle more than any other shape
But I can never draw a perfect one
Sweeping golden leaves in August

Clumsiness is a cute trait until it's time to
Perform open heart surgery or
Decide on a high-precision word choice
Whether I love you the most or a lot
What if one sun is so bright I'm always in its shadow

I am a prodigal daughter
Only homesick in harvest season
Climbing over the wall to a stranger's garden

Summer Night City

Nobody sleeps while catching fire
In the hot glow of the moon
The city is a gilded cage dissolving
An ocean of brilliance marred with bits of asphalt

A girl flies through a forest aflame
A basket of cherries on her handlebar
Her bright bell rings into the heat without melody
It is another end of the world

The attendees of the wake lick salt off each other's skin
Delirious with the self-defeating hope of summer
This time the sea will be an impossible blue
And skytrails will spell out love letters

Nothing will burn except for candles stuffed in wine bottles
In someone's beautiful birthday party
The flowers will keep blooming forever
Petrified in technicolour

Mid Year Review

This morning if the bus catches fire
I shall not alight — an angelic pillar
Clenching my teeth into fairy dust
Just to be not here, the false start
Quicksand in my stomach.
My body learns the texture of betrayal
Dancing to its shiversong thrill
I feel wired wrong and volatile
In frequency, stuck between stations
A ghost of two lovesongs
Missing its spine

Cousins

Schoolgirl on the bus running her teeth
Over the hard candy edge of a cavity
There's no connection down here
We pass our time by counting blessings
How many missed calls from mother
She dreads the moment of resurfacing
Sky grey and dense with cement rain
Surrounded by an abundance of exit routes
The cousins all say they are so jealous
She will always have somewhere to go
Some fast-moving thing to speed her along
But she never picks up the phone, too busy
Crawling, hard taste of gravel in her mouth

Eurostar Sale

In another life I'm watching pigeons fight
Over crumbs of pastry by a burning bus
My mouth curling into unfamiliar shapes
My left cortex sapir whorfing libertinisme
These bleak afternoons make a belle bonfire
And inside me it was all a mist a match misstruck
Setting the wrong house all aflame, a smoking lung
Collapsing with revolutionary pretences
Collapsing all the same

Charitable Interpretation

A woman on the street asks for an orange slice of the sky
All I have to offer is a rusty penny with a sanguinary smell
Watch her place it on her tongue and close her mouth
Swallowing with a slot machine click, clover bell clover
Flickering as she walks down the street, acid dissolving
Money into little heat, frost like rat poison in our lungs
Lemon clover clover. Feeding pigeons with french bread
Staring at the iced swan boats, immobile on the surface
Sometimes thawing hurts more than the freezing did
Yet I crave the sun so far beyond lightless fields
Lifting a candle to my lips to lick the flame, small star
Burning through stomach lining, central nervous heating

Colder Light

I have been longing for the soft cloth of autumn
draped over me, the merciful closing of the sun's eye
forgiving what lies beyond light. Winter brings no rest
banging on my windows at three in the morning

Visions of a drowning man
smashed glass and voice
nightmares of being watched
a hard fear plays my heart
so I dream of yielding
bending under dusk-weight
into mass graves of August flowers

It is only safe to speak when I'm alone
only safe to feel when I'm not here
Begging for someone to write me
a role I only want in the flesh

You can have me if you destroy me, is what I'm saying
but I don't want you to listen.
I want you to hurt me like a natural disaster
but reality destroys fiction.

Tell me another bedtime story, spell it on my back
with that cold steel buckle of your belt. Write it again
and again, a fading armistice, easy as a ragged breath.

Ĭ thought
Ĭ want to
see the sea

I got home late one night, a little flushed from the third vodka coke John had bought me now that he was finally unskint, and found myself face to face with a ghost trapped in a cheap picture frame.

In a world of a billion blue pixels, a badly blurred woman opened her mouth in a silent scream. I could almost hear the rain drenching her, soaking into her short black hair, running down her nude body in violent rivulets.

Jun must have put it up earlier that day. The sole nail on the wall of the hallway had been bare ever since we moved in months ago, begging to be covered with something, but both of us had lacked the initiative until now. I couldn't begin to imagine why he had chosen this picture in particular, but the most important thing was that the nail finally had something to hold. It made me feel slightly sentimental.

I found him frying some eggs in the kitchen, shirtless back turned to me. He didn't notice me walking in --- only the strawberry moon glared at me through the open window. I wanted to lick the bend of his spine, watching the muscles shift underneath, but that could wait until after dinner.

'Why did you put up that picture?' I tried to ask, but the sound of the oil and the fire overpowered my words. I took a step closer and placed my hand on his shoulder, probably giving him a little shock, but he didn't show it. 'Why did you put up that picture?' I repeated much closer to his ear.

'Dunno.'

'Is it a ghost?'

'What? No. It's a still from a film.'

'Not a ghost film?'

'I don't think so. Do you want some eggs?'

'Sure.'

'How was your day?' Jun asked as we sat on the floor, our knees touching under the low coffee table.

'Pretty uneventful.'

'You're back so late again.'

'I'm sorry. It was somebody's birthday, so I had to go for drinks. I know, it's always somebody's birthday. What about you?'

'It was nobody's birthday.' Jun pierced an egg yolk with

his spoon and watched its dome collapse in a puddle of mercurial orange, soaking the rice underneath. 'I mopped the floor and hung the picture. I had a feeling you'd be home late, so I put off making dinner.'

I stopped myself from asking if he had looked for jobs, but I wasn't sure what else to talk about. In the corner of the room, a jazz record was spinning mercifully.

We ate the food without saying any more words. When it was finished, Jun made a movement to get up and clear the dishes. I stopped him by climbing into his lap and leaning forward until his back was flat against the floor.

Straddling his thighs, I wrapped the fingers of my right hand very lightly around his neck and dragged the nails of my left hand slowly across his bare stomach. When I reached the band of his underwear, his Adam's apple moved hard against the base of my thumb. My own throat constricted in anticipation.

What I longed for was the moment I could hear him stop thinking. I'd done this enough times that the trigger sequence of my hands felt nearly pre-programmed, but not quite. There was always an unexpected detour, a distraction or disturbance of sorts, either exterior or interior. I could work around it, creating a new force field of my own, a slow glow of adoration.

Eventually, the harsh noise in his mind would clear out and

transfer into something far sweeter on his tongue. I liked pushing down on his stomach to anchor him when he lost himself, feeling his heartbeat all the way in the pit of his belly.

'The floor is very clean,' I whispered into his ear.

That night, I dreamed of an empty parking lot in blue. The air wasn't clear --- it shimmered with a static I could almost taste, although I wasn't really there. It was the scream of invisible cicadas enclosing the space. Soon the sky itself opened its mouth. Metallic sheets of rain fell and glitched and swirled around my absent body. I felt like someone was watching me, eyes on me like nails on a chalkboard.

When my alarm woke me, the golden sunlight streaming in seemed fake. I wondered if Jun was dreaming in the same colour. It was a terribly sad shade of blue.

Suddenly I was struck by a fear that he'd hung the image as a warning sign, a declaration of ill intent, a suicide note. It was hard not to read too much into it, but the peacefulness of his sleeping face reassured me. I pressed a lipstick print on it before leaving for work and hoped he wouldn't turn to face the other way on the cream-coloured pillow.

I'd always thought that the range and intensity of human feeling is quite independent of circumstances --- as long as life is not total physical suffering, it doesn't matter too much whether it is lived in utter luxury or lack of it. Sadness will prevail over some moments, and dissipate in others. I might have felt a pang of betrayal whenever the supermarket was out of bananas, but my great grandmother probably never had nor longed for one. I liked to imagine her savouring the taste of beetroot pickles in the darkness of an underground cellar, cutting the browned part off a half-shrivelled apple in midwinter, convincing herself that it would all be worth it in harvest season, when the glory of golden damson flesh would stick to her palms as she ate her way through the garden like a small animal. She would have recognised the feelings of desire or delight or disappointment that course through my nervous system. I believed that all feelings are old feelings, and felt comforted by their eternity.

Still, it was evident that some people felt more violently than others. At times I wished I were one of them, simply because I was tired of dragging my own dull self around, even though I understood that this blunt ache of emptiness was probably easier to endure than the sharp pain of overwhelming sensation. I'd never understood people who killed themselves because I'd never particularly wanted to either live or die, and perhaps this was for the best, a life within a sensible scale.

On the train, I had a habit of looking at people's faces and wondering if they were currently experiencing an emotion or if their minds were occupied by thoughts untethered to any noticeable agitation of the heart. I was pretty sure most of my assessments were incorrect, yet I kept making them. Most people had a restlessness that seemed to border on distress, but occasionally I was struck by the saintliness of a person smiling, eyes closed without tension, even as they held onto a hanging strap with bodies pressing into them from all sides. Maybe those saints were suffering immensely and self-soothing with elaborate fantasies of blowing it all up the next day.

'Did you know,' John said to me when I walked into the office.

'What?'

'I already forgot.'

'Oh.'

'Good morning.'

My desk was slathered in buttery sunlight, and I sat down and opened my laptop with a little sigh. I always moved slowly in the mornings, even though I knew I was only taking on a debt of calm that often forced me to work unpaid overtime.

During the meandering morning, I fantasised about setting up an emotions trading scheme and absorbing the excess tears of others with my surplus quota of unspent emotion.

That was the kind of thing I couldn't say out loud, except maybe to Jun. He would understand, although we were not the same. When I first met him, I thought the inside of him was a fading watercolour like mine, but in time I saw that subdued sky was troubled by jagged slashes of ink, gleaming.

'Can you do it,' John said, suddenly standing next to me.

'What?'

'The meeting.'

'Yeah, of course.'

'Good. I knew I could count on you.'

I got home late that evening, but slightly earlier than the night before. The meeting had overrun, like they always did.

The lights were off in the hallway, so I turned them on. I saw Jun's face in the blue picture frame, and my heart leaped. A trick of the light. I flicked the switch off and on again, but the interlude of darkness did not change the image. I took a breath and walked into the living room, which was empty. The floorboards were still very clean, and I lay down and closed my eyes.

What I felt must have been an old feeling, but I could not

name its colour.

Forest Angel

A cruelly lukewarm
Summer submerged in
An acid bath of midnight
Blue hydrangeas
My face will not stop burning

Late Spring

Neriums in bloom
MRI beats, fingers in my hair
A dead mother awash in obscenity
I pixelated her name for decency
But her face was there for all to see

Did you know that latex is an opium too
Fought over by faceless men
Their strings pulled by the sun
The room filled with mechanical laughter
Nobody wanted to stop and stare
At the imaginary panic button

I wore white to the elevator
And thought about slashing my throat
I called my mother instead
To tell her about the neriums in bloom
Although I could not name them
I think she knew what I was talking about

The snow was still
Higher than a tall child
A protective layer of sorts
Hospital gown, scissors on my brow
Nothing was in bloom

Falling Man

You talk to the darkroom parts of me
Every word an antiecho
Blue baby latched at my breasts
Bruised thighs soaked in a stop bath
No god shall fill me. What am I empty for?
Washing my face in stagnant pools of amniotic fluid
Defiling the womb defiles the self. A bridge bound to rot
The flood has no concept of your ego
How heavy are you while falling through?

Hells In Bottles

We have chosen different theatres of violence
with shared principles: Sacred is to have heart.
The sight of fake blood disgusts both of us.
What makes you dangerous
is mercury running through your veins
I am the least dangerous thing in the world
leaving the hotel empty-handed, gone
silent, fireworks in black water.

A man for me is shadowplay
overlay of phantoms
guarding secret shames
in trigger sequence

You only pick the battles I can't fight
My tears keep taking me by surprise
Is it the touch for touch, the gentle gesture
Violated by the clarity of memory
How you hold me and slam the door
Cut kisses on my paper skin
My glitching code of honour

Rush Hour

Coagulating formulations of faith
The grain of her skin was all analog she
Felt love in her fingertips felt smoke in her lungs
In every chamber of her heart an unmade bed
And an empty chair beside it, she slept without stories
Sinking into the black of her eyelids so formless
Rising from the deep, creatures that leave no trace
In memory, notes that ring out and fade
Into everlasting frequency, head full of traffic
Walking between cars that shine like hard-shell insects
Ugly gemstones, catching glimpses of daughters
Taking cat naps in the backseat, hiding from their nausea
Spines curled in a question mark, how long is this rehearsal
Will I still fit in that silence, the wombless womb of real sleep
She felt the damp of their hair through window glass
And imagined a small comb in her hand,
In her mother's hand, untangling the days
Their eyes watering with the force of it
The merciless pulling-apart. The traffic would not stop
The daughter's face hidden in half-sleep
Her mother's comb buried in a winter field
So far away, through the formless deep
She'd sink down to that frozen earth
To claw at it, pull a sword of myths
But the chair was empty, without stories

Butoh Class

A decade of silence breaks water
You must walk with your eyes closed
Accustomed to the totality of darkness
Let eternities pass in a new womb

Forget a minute consisting of sixty seconds

What is any of this but a death spiral
veiled in the ticking of hearts & watches
upon tanned wrists, the hypnotism
of plastic metronomes.

On stage
every limb an oar
rippling the time

a Horizon Sheds Itself

Vipers cross the July soil with impunity
through gilded barley stretching to infinity
each muscular twist of scales a lightning bolt —
beware of the snakes, now, stay out of the tall hay —
won't you listen, God damn it? Don't you know
what's the worst that can happen, child,
can't you see it right before your eyes, open, closed?
There is no mercy in this world. The sun is too high
and the work is undone. I dream of gathering
your small bodies into my arms, a kinetic lullaby,
gentler than I ever knew how to be.

I will watch you walk far beyond these fields
over the snakes. One day I will see you bury
their hides so deep into the bloodied earth

Lines in The Sand

After watching you shatter   pink magic sand on bathroom tiles
I search myself for a splinter   a shadow at the foot of her bed
We fell the same distance   in the night sometimes she dials
yet only I remain whole.   breathing hard. all unsaid
I possess a strange resistance. behind the house the woods are thin
Is it a loophole in my soul?   exposing   within

Juniper

Have the instructions been unclear
Streets green in the wake of my sister
The mermaid in a freefall aerobus
Red rope of fate bundled on the floor
All knotted up waiting for a sailor
Ocean wedding caked with dirt
Today the silk has a sandpaper feel
Clinging to my fingers thick as blood
We search every inch of the sea beach
For fish scales the tide brings in minor key

GGGiRL!

Call me pretty and I'll cry
blood on cue, just for you
Dreams of slaughter
Violate me. Elevate me

I take it so well, flying high
Chem pearl on my tongue
Read me hagiography
Breed me violent sleep

My favourite thing in the world is fucking
a raging misogynist
schizoid soft femicidal
pillow talk

Butcher me harder
I'm less pink inside
Glitter-guts
Reform tomorrow

MaTERiaL

We have requested an extraction of the self
Nobody is willing to work with such volatile material
Worth not very much at all
And the truth is there is a surplus of self
Supply far exceeding demand
Sometimes the self likes to be buried in sand or wet autumn leaves
Pretending it knows how to participate
Most of the time it hides behind barbed wire fences
In tall buildings whose concierges make no eye contact
Its biographical details blinking on lidless screens
We have requested a metamorphosis of the self
No instructions have been provided
Like glued moths we stick to the hands of the clock
Hoping our combined weight will force them to slow down
Or even change direction

FLOATING

Red threads laid out underground
Humming electrical cables
Breathe in enflamed firs,
Oxides of nitrogen, greetings
How was your day & look
At this surgical cut of my life
Floating cups of coffee, flowering trees
A new dusk descending on my hips
Fast frequency response lovers
Supercharged by distance
Attachment survive misplacement
What a thrill, knowing you exist
Somewhere, doing something
Most of it left unsaid
I prefer you this way

Revisionist Histories of Love

Molly rolls the saran wrap tighter and tighter around my body until I'm a hothouse of sweat and laboured breath.

My grandmother was born in nineteen-sixty-one and spent endless childhood mornings in the back of a boat, drowsily watching her uncles haul dragnets across the blue. Now she's eighty-three, and the plastic far outweighs the fish. I heard that in a news documentary a while ago, and my grandmother's small form floating atop a mass of fins surged to my mind. I hope this factoid has not been brought to her attention; I will never tell her, because it would be too cruel. I am old enough to understand that growing up means losing things, one after another, and gradually learning to let go, arms wide open. But I am thinking about reverse-embracing houses, seasons, lovers, not life itself. Breathless waters suffocate the heart.

The billions of microplastics I have swallowed coalesce into a hard lump beneath my jaw. My mouth makes a slight choking sound, and Molly lifts her hand on autopilot, making sure the wrap stays around my lips. This is supposed to be a meditation, not a suicide attempt.

'How does it feel?' she asks.

'Good,' I sigh. 'Safe.'

Molly is watching me like a bird of prey, licking her lips. My skin strains against the tight encasing of plastic.

'Would you still like to..'

I nod, and she smiles at me. I can't feel her grip on my arms, lowering my body all the way down, and it's disorienting. I squeeze my eyes shut and pretend I am nowhere. Once my limbs are set against the floor, Molly undoes a bundle of coarse hemp rope and starts creating a little prison for my body. Maximum security. She is so strong, working around the mass of my body, twisting it into a constellation of knots.

Once the groundwork is done, she attaches the ties atop my chest to a meat hook on the ceiling and begins to pull me up slowly, slowly, a soft burden. If only we could be standing in a lake instead, pure like an Evian advert. She stops to consider the weight, and I wonder if she's giving up on me, but she doesn't. The earth lets me go.

Doubly sheathed, I observe the scene from afar. In the year of my grandmother's birth, Yuri Gagarin said being in space feels like suspension. While in its orbit, he fell in love with the earth and felt a strong urge to protect it. He was so small.

Underneath me, Molly's bedroom, her wiry body, everything spins in soft focus. From the way she looks up at my face, I can see that she is in love with me. Her fingers caress my bound breasts so carefully, as though she were afraid of hurting me with her touch, as though I couldn't take her knife through the hemp and the plastic unoffended. She keeps rocking me gently, gently, my watery friend.

I was expecting to enjoy this feeling, but it's dreadful. Nothing like leaping into a darkening sky.

Soft Core

I suck my lips thin, unsure
If dignity is a lie or a fantasy, if it's wrong
When I indulge my perversions
Other people bite their lips & teeth
Anticipating a devouring,
never to come, which is the point
You need the right glasses to see
My prescription is pink film rosy
A virgin soul satisfied by constant gesture
The metal eye caressing metaphysically
If you touch my pink skin it won't be cinematic

Come Spring

Organising goodbye letters in order of finality
In the vast void deck of the night
She wanted only what she could have
To seduce an illiterate flower
The ease did not remove the sin of it
Petals burst through the earth with violence
Scarring the ground with such innocence
Nothing like her yellow lust for the sun

Deep in the garden tearing the weeds apart
Roots and all, shredding their colour to pieces
There was no other way. How the mud ended
Up around her neck like a string of dirty jewels
She didn't know, discarding silent limbs
All around her kingdom in warning

Underneath her desire
A green prison
Dry spring
Clay crumbling
Before
The shape of beauty
Could emerge

Dues

You will not reach the end
On bruised knees. Stop your crawling
A north star explodes

Let the wind lick your wounds
Bind you to this frozen morning
Raise the red horizon

Girls from nothing & nowhere
Hold inverse currency: keep small
To pay for the love you need

Steal your way through heavy doors
Gather the dust, count its worth
Each day a small ingratitude.

When you tire of equations, draw
The queen of spades, a white flag
Speckled with old blood.

Show your hand to the maidens
Waiting with candles in their hair
Milky eyes on silver platters

A house is a thing to live for
Gift of debt, beams of love
Piercing through the heart wall

R A B B i T Y e A R

Sometimes I wake up in the morning I want to play a game
The only rule is I must not say what I mean
Get out of bed when the sun outside is a fat orange
Suck the ash off my fingers for breakfast
The screens all running a battlefield simulation
Being blackened into rubbery nothing because that is the way
A pink glitch explodes the city into petals of pixels, harmless
There is someone waiting for you behind the wardrobe
Longing to take you for a dance, oh sweet princess
Do you remember when we sat in the client meeting together
The way your nails gripped the soft flesh of my thighs
I knew you were the best dressed little animal in the whole
    corporation
Of people running around doing important things with strings
    of numbers
And language, but what is the language of animals?
In this way we can speak to each other. I lie in the tall grass and
    wait
You feel the tension, fist in your lungs. Clench it. Do you
    believe in
Victory?

eVeLYn

I watch you read my
twice inked flickerface
sick December sun

You like your wounds rare
icegaze-thawed, yielding
clouds of stupid silence

Instead of drowning I kiss
your whisper: 'I've got you'
like the water
wouldn't carry me anyway

Cast the dragnet of your sun
kill my wet shadowsorrow

MUD

Once I saw the path laid out
In the bend of a spine
Now I don't know up from down
My hand burns the hollow
Charred cartographies

Toward the blank spaces of the everyday where
Suddenly something is there, a quiet
Gravity uncalled — take the earthquake into you
Bury it deep in the heart-land epicentre
Hold the handle of a worn-out leash
Stitched with crimson thread of life
Watch everything move but you
A centrifugal slow dance

My stage knife spills thick ink
Carving murders out of thin air
Shadows move slowly
Bracketed by iron bars

The point of the needle knows where to flesh itself out
Seeking skin with a higher purpose, a language
Of wounds opened into secrets
By the perfect silence of pain
The fade and throb of memory

Is it good to leave no trace on this world
as I tread on its infinite wounds
Is it wicked to plant seeds in a lake of blood
even if the water lilies bloom

STRAYS

Vulnerability is attack surface maximalism
I know the process of love but the object

Wild-eyed in a Chinatown aquarium
Catch of factory-farmed feelings

My soiled vessel in this world
Led by your impatient shadow

Down some wine dark alley
The usual please: Recited blindfolded

Oh the object is the mystery

Remember The Herbs My Love

The first film we watched on a hot laptop balanced atop
a tangle of pale legs: Badlands. My heart ached for that
doomed desert love, carving honeymoons from dust:
Sand dunes / Black holes, all must collapse.

How lucky I thought us, existing in pockets of space-
time more easily overlooked.
Unbothered by the world. Squeezed against the wall in
your narrow bed.
I'd kiss the plaster goodnight, grateful
for the slowness of your breath to pacify

my being
condensed
presence. So simple

Gravity got us in the end, too
What I want to remember
Is weightlessness:
My knees against yours
Your arms on my waist
How you held my heaviness,
And I held yours,
diminished.

Sleep Knife

I never dream
sliding knives
viscous black of nights

Sometimes a nightmare
is awakening
blood chafed thighs

Would have said
yes maybe something maybe
sleeping beauty set aflame
learning pyromania

to love it when you make her swallow
pearly aphrodisiacs
fade to black
and back
here

Burning burning
no stakes witch
I don't scream
a real dream
freely given
gift of voice

Moony Meal

How many more worm moons
Will your mealy flesh endure
How many words will you swallow
The mind fills in the blanks between breaths
The heart staggers, staking out territory
Between electric peaks of blue
I learn to enjoy whatever makes me gasp
Whatever is a thrill. Raised in a beehive
She has a honeyed death drive, quick to die
Less eager to kill. We will eat what is left of her.

Mealy Moon

One way or another I will worm myself back in
It will be as easy as fisting a bruised apple
Smashing a mottled sunset into pieces
Of fattened pleasance, a canned flower
Opens for me, so sweet after all these years
Rosy-cheeked breathing into rusted hinges
What I meant back then is no longer in season
I shall take a sickle to the path crowded with roses

Needless

That night made me a silver needle, shy stab-eyes hitting target shiverspine whispers. Not sure if I wanted to be you or see you, gleaming like a Wunderkammer key in a bathroom stall, hiding some unsmiling blonde in a too-tight leopard top. You left my breath locked in to that tremble against the door

Early Breakfast

Miles and miles of unlit railway tracks
eaten up. The night train spills its guts
4 a.m Kunming station iron jaws,
the sky a steel plate stained with dawn
exhalation fog mixing in with
scalding mixian, solace for the shivering
slipping into lobbies with cold marble floors
as if closing my eyes renders me invisible
morning devoured by hungry clouds
Pockets fill with starch of soggy maps
wire mesh streets swallow me, misery
of clogged concrete arteries – somewhere
is a heart, throbbing with warmth
unmeasured by cartographers

SeALaNT

Sound transfers poorly over lakes of hard plastic
how should I know to turn toward the sun
with this cut throat slashed pedicel
I may be out of time, on blades of grass
or below, all at once. You are a cartographer
moving inside a thing of form and direction
carefully drawing hachures and graticules
invisible to me. Blindness to the trajectory of things
may be a symptom of naïveté, stupidity
breeding imagination: I do not know where I am
so I am everywhere, lost and mostly fearless.
Where is the mouth that speaks these words?
I want to tell you I am here sometimes
when you touch me I feel the ground beneath

Long Live Dreamy Doppelgängers

Today I gazed at a tall man wearing a striped shirt in the wine aisle. I thought of the sticky August evening I was so desperate to hear from you I texted, from the relative safety of a homebound train, 'i think i saw you on the street earlier today and i just wanted to say i'm sorry if i accidentally stared at you' even though that was an almost complete lie. I didn't even know what your face should have looked like, on a live dust-speckled street, outside the confines of sleek cyberspace. It was just some guy whose shirt slightly resembled one I had seen you wear on Instagram before. I knew it wasn't you, but it scared me just how much I wanted it to be.

What would I have said to you? The question made me squirm like a teenager in a first-crush inferno: deeply unbecoming. During that bizarre pretend-encounter, the real weight of my desire proved far too much to bear. I had to walk myself into the cool air of a supermarket and swallow a mini bottle of Merlot to calm my shaky hands down. 'sorry i'm being really weird!!!'

'yesterday i saw a girl in the marshes i thought was you, actually,' you responded, and I couldn't help wondering if she really looked like me, or if it was a similar instantly fleeting resemblance, an illusion created by an item of clothing or perhaps simply the colour of her hair ---

What do I look like, in your head, anyway? Good girl / slut / God forbid, a whole person? When it comes to men, I'm far more interested in their predisposition for dichotomy than monogamy. Was I a girl in a Gunne Sax sundress or perhaps tattered fishnets?

In that instance, I cared too little to press for details. I was happy that there was an image of me in your head at all, some form of a presence to project onto reality.

I've had enough of this reality. I wonder if I will ever see you (all of you at once, casting a shadow over me), kiss your eyelids (is that weird?), feel your hands on my neck (while you kiss me back, preferably). Probably not.

What is there to do in this world but kiss or pine for a kiss?

After endless months unkissed, I'm left wondering if that girl in the wetlands --- it doesn't matter if she's real at all --- has had a better run of her luck. I can't see her face: I hope she's smiling. I hope her smile is pressed against a soft mouth, her eyes closed in bliss.

74<

excalibUr

My second heart beats
Only rarely its every
Little red movement
An earthquake that sends fatal
Permafrost fragments flying

My excalibur
A red comb buried too deep
In a frozen field
For the sun to ever thaw
Unpassed by all passing springs

My eldest daughter
Sleeps cradling a splitting axe
The red handle shines
Her dream a song of sorrow
Rising from burial grounds

Blossom

There are lions over the fence believe me
Something devastating in the evening sun on my sheets
Gilded for nothing in particular

I stopped waiting for him. Spring caught my breath
Suddenly there is love everywhere. Everywhere

Her soft hands angling the glass to pour my drink
Golden light. I say our bodies will remember how to stay
On the top thrill dragster of days when they creak into
    motion again. Or if not
I am determined to enjoy the falling, my stomach in
    butterfly knots
And above all I am convinced there will be enough love for
    all of us
Pollen floating in the air. Inhale too hard you might hack
    up your lungs but it's nothing
Dangerous. It doesn't matter if the red is heartbreak or
    hayfever when you walk up the hill &
Witness the blinding blossom of clouds.

SEeD BiRD

Recklessly cross-exchanging keys with neither shame nor secrecy
The metal freezes on my palm like a sparrow I cannot feed
Far from the cold marsh. Grief twice-removed lingers in exhalation

Only on Tuesday morning I was torn apart strip by strip
The skyward-pointed scissors devoured my outlines
I shed petals of plastic and black duct tape

In the video of myself coming undone I was laughing like a child
I was a child watching myself laughing
In that small room overcast by concrete forests

I cut my ribcage open and seeds spill out, but
No winter garden to plant them in. I fill my screens
With timelapses of ugly apples blooming from snowflowers

D o E

I fall asleep to you crying beside me
Wake up to you crying beside me
Eat your tears instead of trying to decipher them

Running down long corridors
Your salt on my tongue
Serve the people. The time is never right

I would squeeze the life out of this afternoon if it made you smile
You always look so harmless after a haircut
I am simply obsessed with historicising things
I really think you should stop spiraling

My boss describes a scent from his childhood
Pressing his thumbs into soft doughy memory
How beautiful to exist in two places at once

When your legs buckled under you
Bambi trembling unto my fingers
Your mouth made the same O of the crying night
And the crying morning, only the sound was so sweet
I think you almost forgot
The other place
The other time
The wetness of your face

This is the only way I want you to lose

top Season

Shivering in a silk slip I feared extinction
A coral reef in place of lungs, mixing red and yellow
Counterstrike, online and inflesh her first question
Was about needles gauges, whether I preferred
The blue or the green, recreationally speaking
I said I never made that choice for myself
But the purpose was drawing not enhancing blood
So any one would do, the purples or the reds even
As our eyes met in confused understanding
A man stood by like a small hand of a clock

ReCoVeRY

Was I better when
There was no prosaic en-
jambment of blood and
Air when I kept my
Colour bright on the inside

With unsteady feet
I must clamber up this hill
Of volcanic ash
The sulphur a bitter song
Inside my ambitious lungs

Caught by a sudden
Hail of rainsoaked sugar cubes
Turns into icing
In his hair the colour of
True and everlasting love

Busy hands tearing
Everything chantilly laced
Chemical compounds
A startlingly delicate
Indestructibility

Antiseptic

Measuring time by the wound
On your stomach, I kiss it
Before opening my eyes

At night I watch its gilding
In the buttery lamplight
Feel the dissipation of danger

The way your skin holds itself
Together with perfect tension
Long after the body heals

February 2012

Shining through cirrocumulus gaps
Deep waters forest hearts
Jungles of machines

Screaming day or night
Houses hours reach toward the stars
Lump of polystyrene I

Crumble alone in a bus station café
Make a black oil puddle on the floor
For the happy ones to drown in

When I was young I hated poems
Strange tricks of language
Now a beautiful worn-out verse I

Lost the engagement ring
Years ago the room suffocates
In its own silence the sun sets

But I'm smiling

StrateGEm

A scorched earth face growing craters
The numbness of my lips the warmth in my belly
This label proves nothing but hells in bottles
Adrift off the desertshore, the circulation of shame
Drowning is a false meditation, seeing underwater
The skin is transparent. The heart is transparent
With every breath it expands, gills of lace
A crushing embrace a soundless explosion
To go beyond the jaws of tectonic plates
To go beyond

Retrograde

What a phenomenal overreaction
To flinch away from the barrel
With the safety still on
She whispers your name
Christening an inbound asteroid
In the starless urn of sky
Black burn for singed lungs
A lustless kiss, shot in the dark
Licks teeth clean of soured love

husk

When she was still alive, my mother loved to dispense life lessons. One of the few I still remember is this: 'Good love is an amulet.' I must have been about fifteen when she said it, while fixing her hair for a rare dinner out with dad. 'When someone loves you well, let that feeling crystallise inside you. Keep it forever. It will protect you from bad love.' I didn't understand what she meant by bad love, and I didn't ask, because I wanted to seem disaffected. Understanding would not have kept me any safer.

The wedding ring I wear around my neck is the antithesis of my mother's amulet. I keep fantasizing about yanking the chain so hard it breaks, but I'm worried my head will come off with it.

'Count them down,' I say to the man lying on the shiny laminate floor of the dungeon, on his back like a red lacquer beetle. My left hand holds a promise, a bamboo cane raised high.

'Yes, mistress.' At the first strike, his whole face scrunches beneath the thick blindfold.

'Twelve … eleven … ten.'

There are metal clips strapped tight into the folds of fat in his back, and he is straining to keep still, but it's a poor attempt. Every strike of mine is followed by a clank of metal against the floor, a pained little yelp as the clips twist deeper in his skin. He is breathing through his nose.

'Stay still now, or I'll whack you over the blindfold and crush your eyes like soft egg whites.' He stops writhing at once. Only his fingertips tremble discreetly.

'Three ... two ...'

I let my rhythm fall a little slack, listening to his inhalations as he thinks it's coming, any second now, the last sweet lick of pain. His shoulders twitch slightly.

My mind wanders to domestic scenes, all the shit I should do before Sylvain gets home, breakfast dishes in the sink and the glowing hollow of the fridge. I wish I could make these men do something more useful instead of draining both our resources, but that would require merging parts of my life anathematic to one another.

'Please, mistress,' the man gasps.

'Do you want me to put you out of your misery, little swine?'

'Yes, please, please,' he whines.

I give him what he wants, and two extra whacks for being annoying. That's the end of our session. I help him up by his shoulders, extract the clips --- slowly, slowly --- and let him admire the angry bite marks in the mirror.

'Have I been a good boy?' he asks nonsensically.

'No, of course you haven't. You're a fucking waste of space. You disgust me.'

I sit down on the leather bench and watch him scutter out of the door, throwing a long-suffering glance at me. He's one of my favourite customers, although it's not saying much.

When I get home, I find moths in the coffee maker. I pull the jar out, hoping they'll stir and flutter away, but they lie silent in their coffin of stained glass.

Sylvain comes in, and the air grows thicker. He sits on the sofa, headphones on, frowning at his phone. I start doing the dishes, and he comes into the kitchen to microwave some leftovers. He doesn't say anything, and I don't say anything, because I don't want to face his lack of response. I look at him and wonder if he can feel my eyes on him. I don't know what cursed him, but his transformation into stone is almost complete.

A couple of hours later, while I'm taking a shower, he walks in on me. 'What's happened to the coffee maker?'

'I threw it away,' I say through the clouded glass door.

'Why?'

'There were dead moths in it.'

'Why didn't you just clean it?'

'We never drink coffee anymore. That's how it ended up moth-ridden in the first place.'

During the first months of our marriage, I brewed a large pot of coffee every morning, and we would finish every last drop of it before work. I remember sitting in his lap, kissing his neck between scalding sips while he read the newspaper. During the first six months he spent in exile from me, assigned to the furthest possible base, a lot of things changed.

Now, Sylvain slides the door open and looks at my body. I wish he would come closer, fully clothed, in the nude, doesn't matter. I wish he would force himself on me. I want to know if the sight of me is making him hard. He fixes his eyes on my face and says: 'Well, that's fucking stupid.'

'Why don't you ever want to drink coffee with me anymore?' I say in that kicked-dog voice which always makes him wince in disgust. Predictably, he turns around and leaves. I wish he'd at least slam the bathroom door, but he closes it very gently. I hear his footsteps echoing in the stairwell as I dry my hair.

There is nothing to do, so I go to bed and close the black-out curtains. At some point in the night, I stir --- Sylvain's weight is on top of me, inside me, his hands pressing down on my ribs.

'You're dangerous,' he says, dripping sweat over me.

'Why?' I say in a small voice. I think I am the least dangerous person in the world.

'Because you'd let me do anything to you, wouldn't you. I don't trust you to ever tell me what you're really thinking.'

I'm drowning in these words, more water to the depths already within me --- there is simply not enough air to breathe and respond. Sylvain's hands move to my throat, absolving me from any expectation of reply.

'I wish you'd talk to me,' he growls. 'I really don't know what your fucking problem is.'

His anger is a flower sewed shut, the stitch-seams glistening with old blood. For years, I have been trying to tear it open with my bare hands, expose the rotting core of it to the sun.

Before they enter the dungeon, my clients fill out a checklist of the things they want to do in session. Ticking boxes is the antithesis of real desire. It's sad, but comforting too --- who wants to confront what they truly want? The real function of these shopping lists for unattainable things is to protect my clients from their own hearts.

My blade carves wet streaks into the skin beneath Mr. W's shoulder blades, and he screams despite knowing you get what you pay for, here, unearned insults and butter knives dipped in a bucket of ice. Zero death, zero rebirth. I keep thinking of those dead moths.

'Aren't you sick of living in this disgusting skin? I'm doing you a favour, peeling it off you,' I whisper. 'What's beneath is so much prettier. Will you show me all of it?'

Mr. W. whines something unintelligible in response. 'What?' I say. 'I asked you a fucking question.'

'Yes, mistress.'

'That's better.' I make an X-shaped slash on his lower back.

He's not crying out this time, just breathing hard. With the water beneath his shoulder blades absorbed into his sweaty skin, and the new puddle on his lower back starting to evaporate, he is becoming fully disillusioned.

'I'm scared,' Mr. W. sniffles. I get up and walk circles around his bound body. 'I'm scared,' he repeats, keeps repeating it until I step on his fingers and he screams. Nothing breaks. I'm so bored of fake fear.

'It wasn't in the --- ' he says half an hour later, unbound and suited up.

'Excuse me?'

'I didn't know you were going to hurt my fingers.' He waves his wrist limply, as though his whole hand were broken. What a joke. 'It wasn't on the list.'

'I'm sorry,' I say.

'Please don't do that again.'

'Of course. I do apologise.' It was a gift he did not deserve.

Sylvain doesn't know about my job, and I'm not sure why I haven't told him. It's been three months since they sacked me, but he thinks I'm still teaching most afternoons. I spend hours upon hours imagining what could happen if I came clean: him bashing my face in and barricading me into the bedroom, or laughing at me and finding the whole thing unremarkably banal, or responding with weeks of hostile silence. I know the last scenario is the most likely, and it's what I dread more than anything. I'm not scared of his anger. Without it I feel as good as dead.

The task of secret-keeping is an enjoyable one. I hold them close to my skin as though they were my amulet, my life suspended mid-air, crystallised into some dark and shimmering thing. I do not tell my husband, and he never asks. I wash my obscene work clothes in the launderette and keep them in the dungeon lockers. My colleagues know which topics not to broach. My clients never touch me. 'How was school?' Sylvain will ask me, when he's feeling gentle, and I will sigh and shake my head and say 'The students are too loud.' Sylvain will shake his head right back and berate me: 'You should discipline them better. Stop being a doormat.'

Stop being a doormat. I've lost count of how many times he's said those words to me, twisting the knife. How many times I've begged him to walk over me, crush my bones, set me free. I can never reach him.

I know it's not a scapegoat I need, but a scalpel, to cut all the horrible dead matter off my heart.

My newest client is hard to read. The first reason I should have refused to see him: he didn't fill out the list, which breaks the very first rule on my booking site. The familiarity of his name seduced me. He used to be the top of his English class, eight years ago. That's the second reason I should have cancelled his reservation. Instead, I am transfixed by the way he glances at me over the slope of his narrow shoulder. 'Turn around,' I say, having ordered him to undress. 'Sit down.'

'I knew it was you, miss,' Thomas says, nervously tapping the arm of the leather chair. 'I recognised your hands.'

'What a disturbing thing to say.'

'I'm sorry. I know there's something wrong with me.'

'Well, you have come to the right place to deal with that. What exactly is wrong with you?'

I wonder if he's playing a different game, trying to humiliate me by exposing some pathological desire for schoolboys. If that's the case, it says a lot about him and very little about me. I have never even considered ---

'I used to always fantasise about you, miss,' he says, staring at his bare feet. 'In class. And after.'

'You were a teenager. It's not abnormal to feel that way. But that was years ago. Surely you have moved on to other fantasies?'

'Of course,' Thomas says, a defensive note slipping into his voice. 'I've had girlfriends my age. I've tried a lot of things. But I can't deny it. Sometimes, I still think about you.'

'When you think about me, what am I doing to you?'

'You're punishing me.' He locks eyes with me, becoming less demure by the second.

'How? What have you done to deserve it?'

'You've caught me stealing your underwear.'

'Where? At school?'

Thomas nods. 'I found a pair of panties in your pencil drawer.'

'Oh. I didn't know you were such a disgusting boy,

rummaging around my private possessions.'

'The panties were black and all bunched up, so I didn't notice until I unfolded and smelled them. But when I did, I realised they weren't clean. I went crazy for your scent.' He looks at me with a challenge in his eyes. 'What would you have done if you'd caught me doing that, all the way back then?'

'Nothing at all,' I say. If my response disappoints him, he doesn't show it. 'I would've bought a new pair of panties. You were just a dumb teenager.'

'And now?'

'I know you haven't just come here to confess. What kind of a punishment do you think you deserve?'

Thomas opens his mouth but doesn't say anything. It doesn't matter --- I know exactly what to do.

He doesn't make a sound when I blindfold him and strap his limbs to the chair. It's only when I squeeze his head into the mask that he starts to whine a little, straining against the leather. The sincerity of his fear thrills me like nothing else. For him to come here, a blank page of a notebook to let me rewrite my own past and his, is an indulgence neither of us have earned. The latex clings to his mouth so prettily.

'Why would you think you deserve to breathe in my scent like that? Why would you think you deserve to breathe at all? Perverts like you are a waste of space.'

'Miss,' he whispers through the mask. 'Are you going to kill me?'

'I don't want to be here with your body,' I say. 'You can breathe through it. Slowly, slowly.' I place my hand on his stomach, reassuring. 'Slowly,' I repeat, but his breathing only becomes more shallow. 'Come on,' I say. 'You can do it.' I look at my wristwatch. After just two minutes under the hood, he is starting to hyperventilate. It's pathetic.

'I see you are too weak to take your punishment.'

'I'm sorry, miss.'

'Don't worry, there are other ways I can make you pay for it. I will release you in thirty seconds.'

My eyes flick between the small hand of my watch and Thomas' Adam's apple, straining as he tries to swallow air. Without warning, his arms go limp, and I rush to yank the hood off his head. His mouth is slack, his eyelids closed without tension. I press my index finger against his neck and find no rush of blood under the skin. He won't inhale any of the air I breathe through his dead lips.

At first, a rush of anger overtakes me. This must be some kind of a cruel joke, arranged as a childish revenge for my earlier indifference. Death possessed him so easily, I wonder if he was fully alive to begin with.

I sit on the floor and stare at his face, bathed in the garish red of the dungeon, expecting him to wake and reveal the trick up his sleeve. He looks oddly unchanged by death. I feel a strange kinship between us: both of our lives may have been suspended long before they ended, like moths under glass. I kiss his eyelids and leave him strapped in the chair, an ornament of fearless desire.

When I get home, it's already dark. Sylvain is sitting on the sofa, watching TV on mute. 'You're late,' he says when I enter the living room. His eyes widen when he looks up at me. 'What's happened to you?'

I walk to him, grab the back of his head and pull him upwards into a rough kiss.

'I broke something,' I say, letting go of his head.

'What do you mean?'

I can only smile at him. My whole body is shaking, but I feel good, so sharp and light, a solar flare. I push my husband into the bedroom and fuck him like I've never fucked him before, until a loud knock interrupts me.

'Ssh, my love, I'll get it,' I say, draping myself in a gauze-thin dressing gown. I close the bedroom door behind me.

'Ms. Wylie?' a woman in uniform says.

'Yes,' I say, beaming at her. 'I was expecting you.' The night air crackles around me like a chrysalis, unstatic, moving me toward something unseen at last.

aCKnOWLeDgE-MenTs

a HoRizOn SheDS iTSeLF :: *ApocAlypsE ConFidentiAl*

BLOSsOm :: *biTTeR fRuiT ReVieW*

THE DEBUtaNtE :: *sARkA*

dUES :: *AuGmeNT ReVieW*

fLoating :: *RiALTo*

GgGirL!!!, mUd, seEdBiRd :: *SpAmZiNe*

hUsK :: *boDy fLuiDs*

LiNeS iN tHe SaNd :: *ReSuRRecTionS*

LoNg LiVe DrEaMy dopPeLgäNgERs :: *fFRAiD*

MeaLy MoON :: *AWAy wiTh wORD.*

ReMemBeR tHe hErBs mY LoVe :: *miNiSkiR*

Milton Keynes UK
Ingram Content Group UK Ltd.
UKHW011721020824
446420UK00012BA/146